WICKED PASSIONS

Glennoe Highlanders #1

NICOLA DAVIDSON

WICKED PASSIONS © Nicola Davidson
First Edition: January 2021
ISBN: 9780473729714 (Paperback)
Editing: Lopt and Cropt Editing Services
Cover: Dar Albert at Wicked Smart Designs

AUTHOR'S NOTES

In real life, the branch of the MacDonald clan near the MacIntyres lived at Glen Coe. To avoid confusion with Glennoe, I changed to Carnoch. (Upper and Lower Carnoch are roads in Glencoe village.)

While cunt and fuck may sound modern, they are both ancient words and the meaning of either has not changed. Cunt was first recorded in England in 1230, a street in the red light district of Southwark, London (Gropecuntelane!) It was commonly used and appeared in both dictionaries and medical texts. Fuck was first recorded in Scotland in 1500 as part of a 'flyting' duel (a verbal smackdown battle) between leading poets William Dunbar and Walter Kennedy in the court of James IV.

Textbooks/sites/articles/ I used in my research:

A Curious History of Sex, by Dr. Kate Lister
    Scotland: A Concise History by Fitzroy Maclean
    The Sword's Path – expert demonstrations of longsword fighting techniques on YouTube

Fighting to Win: the art of sword combat in the early modern period by Danièle Cybulskie

Sword fighting and training basics for beginners

www.swordscholar.com

www.thearma.org

www.medievalwarfare.info/weapons

Highland Games traditions

Archery by Paul E. Klopsteg

List of herbs in the National Library of Medicine herb garden

Africans at the court of James IV by Jennifer Melville

www.stirlingcastle.scot

www.undiscoveredscotland.co.uk/stirling/stirlingcastle

To you—may you find the great love(s) of your life and live happily ever after

CHAPTER 1

Stirling Castle, Scotland, September 1504

No one relished the downfall of a wayward woman like a group of wealthy old men.

Lady Isla Sutherland lifted her chin against the malicious smirks and cold sneers arrowing her way from the courtiers in the lavish royal presence chamber. She had broken their rules, been caught, and now would pay the price: her greatest joys torn away. Henceforth, the blood-heating thrill of steel kissing steel as she vanquished an opponent with her longsword...forbidden. The freedom of linen shirt and woolen hose over itchy velvet gown and heavy gable hood...forbidden.

Nothing could adequately express her fury and frustration. Her despair. But a swordfighter understood the value of strategic retreat as well as advance when important decisions were to be made. Especially when standing in front of a man who held the power of life or death; their anointed sovereign, King James IV of Scotland.

"You sent for me, Your Grace?" said Isla as she sank into a deep curtsy.

James leaned back on his carved oak chair, bejeweled fingers tapping his knee as he studied her. The king wasn't a tall man, nor brawny, his dark brown hair rested fashionably on his shoulders, and he wore well-tailored clothing made of costly fabrics from France. But foes underestimated him at their peril, for James had proven himself both a brilliant scholar with an uncommon gift for languages and a brave, ruthless warrior on the battlefield. He had to be; each day forced to wrangle a spoilt fourteen-year-old wife in Margaret Tudor, her wily father King Henry across the border in England, the changeable French, volatile Scots nobles, and clans who were ever eager to fight one another.

Right now, James looked weary. Understandable when he'd only just returned to Stirling after quelling a border rebellion. This was probably the last matter he wished to pass judgment on, but her wretched clan had demanded an audience—not even the king would risk offending the powerful Earl and Countess of Sutherland.

"Lady Isla," he said with a faint sigh. "What am I to do with a troublemaker who tells her family she travels to the holiest place in Scotland to learn pious ways, and instead disguises herself as a lad to hone sword fighting skills under the tutelage of my champion?"

Isla bit her lip. Now was not the time for a jest about applause. Or to point out that she had been the great Sir Lachlan Ross's best student by far, proving beyond all doubt a lass could wield a sword equal to any lad. The humiliating truth was, her grand plan to triumphantly return from St. Andrews to the north as a fierce and skilled warrior like her father and brothers, had failed. Instead, she would remain the unwanted seventh child with the strange name. The annoyance. The burden.

Worse still, she had caused strife for those who deserved it least.

Sir Lachlan had seen through her disguise, as had his sweet wife Lady Marjorie and their fiery lover Lady Janet Fraser. But all three had kept her secret, challenging her to work harder and be better, and she'd thrived. Until the fateful day a damned rabbit bounded into the ring and tripped her. Falling awkwardly had dislodged her wig and padding, and the viciousness from the lads at discovering a woman had bested them so often had been terrifying. Only Sir Lachlan's intervention saved her life.

"Please, Your Grace," said Isla. "Do not punish others for my deeds. There are none better than Sir Lachlan, Lady Marjorie, and Lady Janet in the realm save yourself."

James nodded. "I know. That is why I ponder what must be done with you and not them. How old are you now? Nineteen or twenty summers?"

"Twenty," she replied cautiously.

"Hmmm. Clearly you are ill-suited for a nunnery. But I cannot allow valuable heiresses to run wild, therefore the best solution is to find you a husband. At once."

No!

While she'd known this would probably be the outcome, it still struck like a blow. The sound of ribald cheers, stomping feet, and gleeful chatter exploding in the presence chamber only rubbed salt into the wound. Two-faced hypocrites. These men would condemn her all day, but that wouldn't stop a single one angling for her substantial dowry and an alliance with the Sutherlands. They would gain everything from the union and she would gain nothing; certainly not love or passion or the indulgence to continue what brought her joy.

This might have been easier to bear if she didn't know that some marriages were happy. But she'd seen couples who were tender. Who accepted and supported each other fully, and scampered away to a bedchamber to indulge their lusts whenever they could. Saints alive, she'd even witnessed a *trio* who did this, so marriages could be exceedingly successful even when unconventional. Bah. In this so-called enlightened time, why did noble daughters still have to be pawns in the careless games of powerful men?

Why could she not decide her own destiny?

Her stomach roiling with hurt and anger, Isla glanced around the presence chamber, searching for a friendly face to bolster her spirits. She certainly wouldn't get that from her family; her older brothers and sisters, and their spouses, had stayed away claiming they were too mortified by her conduct to come to court. In truth she wished her mother and father had abandoned her also, for then she wouldn't be subjected to their icy wrath each day.

In this second painful defeat, she was truly alone.

Isla forced herself to respond. "I will obey my king and wed as you wish."

"Good," said James with a faint smile. "Then I say—"

"Your Grace!"

All heads turned to see Lady Janet barrel her way through the crowd and curtsy. The bold redhead was perhaps the most infamous woman in Scotland, once the king's longtime mistress, still his beloved friend. Only she would dare to interrupt a royal decree.

James raised an imperious eyebrow. "Something to say, Jannie?"

She grinned. "Always, my king. I wonder if Lady Isla has

had sufficient opportunity to meet men of suitable rank and fortune. I am a firm advocate for marital joy; and as the whole realm knows you to be a gallant, perhaps you might grant a wild but *loyal* subject the boon of an occasion here at court to form an attachment."

Occasion.

The word turned over in Isla's mind. What she indeed required was time, and a far better selection of potential husbands than the rotten weasels on offer in this chamber.

A grand feast? No. Too short.

Accompanying the king and queen on a royal progress? No. Too costly.

A tourney?

Isla's heart leaped. Such an event would bring together many men. Strong, salt of the earth warriors who might even admire her gift with a sword. In that group, surely at least one with a good and faithful heart. And skilled at bedsport...

She took a deep breath. "Your Grace, I humbly suggest a tourney."

Gasps echoed around the presence chamber. The stares of the courtiers grew even more disapproving. Yet Lady Janet winked and the king looked...*interested*.

"A tourney?" he mused as he adjusted his heavy purple mantle. "Go on."

"If it pleases you," Isla said slowly. "Send word to the four corners of Scotland that a great royal tourney is to be held. All who enter must be of suitable rank, with a squire to assist. The prize would be...my hand in marriage and all that entails."

Silence greeted her announcement, surely the longest in history. But with her entire future at stake, she forced her gaze to remain on the king.

Eventually, James nodded. "I know my queen would enjoy

such a spectacle. And there are many in my realm who would value the chance to win the hand of such a fair maiden."

Isla nearly snorted. The king was a gallant, but she held no illusions over her charms or lack thereof. Unlike her mother and sisters, all flaxen-haired, buxom beauties, she had her sire's pitch-black curly hair and moss-green eyes. She was neither tall nor short, with narrow hips, coltish limbs, and breasts barely big enough to fill a bodice. Yet as she well knew, her looks were by the by. It was money and an alliance that mattered, and the last Sutherland heiress would tempt even a reluctant suitor.

"Thank you, Your Grace," she said politely.

James stood and clapped his hands together. "Let it be known...a week hence, Stirling shall host a grand tourney open to all unwed men ranked knight, lord, or laird. There'll be five events, determined by me. The victor wins Lady Isla as his wife, and shall receive her dowry, the friendship of the Sutherland clan, and a gift of cloth from the royal household. I look forward to an event celebrating the best of Scotland. That is all."

Isla curtsied again, near-giddy with anticipation. While it would take a miracle for a handsome, honorable man to enter a tourney without knowing the events, *and* be skilled at them all, *and* have good fortune throughout, at least she now had a sliver of hope for a happy future.

Far, far better than no hope at all.

Glennoe Castle, on the shores of Loch Etive
Western Highlands

Failure.

As he stared out the second-floor window of the small stone castle he called home, the word pounded Callum MacIntyre's head like a battering ram at the gates. In the past, when the cares of being a young laird threatened to overwhelm him, he'd been comforted by this view: the cold, deep waters of the sea loch, and the craggy, imposing presence of Ben Cruachan, the mountainous guardian of the glen.

Not anymore.

The coffers were nearly empty; the weaving house—source of most of the clan's income—razed to the ground in a brutal raid; and the mighty neighboring clan, the devil-spawned Campbells, continued to circle and swoop like a golden eagle toying with a plump field mouse.

Since his reckless father's death six months ago, Callum had tried his best to heal the breaches, to make peace and expand trade. But he was an oddity in the Highlands: a nondescript laird of twenty-five summers, average height and lean build, fair hair and gray eyes, the reserved scholar who preferred negotiation to swords. His rule had always been precarious. Now it seemed the whispers were growing even louder to get rid of him: *our laird should be a true Highlander. Not a cursed halfling, spawn of an Englishwoman who calls herself healer but is really a witch...*

"Callum. Are ye listening? Now is not the time for daydreaming!"

Stifling a growl at the disrespect, he turned to gaze upon Rory 'Red' MacDonald. Red was pure Highland stock; a tall, strapping, battle-hardened bull with flaming auburn hair. As he was also laird of his clan branch, the son of Callum's aunt, and ten years older, many viewed him as the true leader of the MacIntyre clan.

Callum tried not to hate anyone. But his cousin made it difficult.

"I heard you, Red," he replied evenly. "Once again insisting I wed a MacDonald lass and bring my clan under your protection."

"'Tis the only way! Unless you wish further Campbell evil?"

"It is not *the only way*. Just a plan to ensure my name ceases to exist. And I won't have that, not when we fought so long to be recognized by the king and council and admitted to the Clan Chattan Confederation."

"What a proud fool ye are," said Red, his lips twisting with scorn. "And who will pay for that? Your people. Any more bloodshed will be on your hands."

The sound of pewter goblet slammed onto wooden table made them both jump.

Callum's mother, Maude, glared at her nephew, her violet eyes flashing. It was said a glance from the Lady of Glennoe could welcome a soul into paradise or purgatory; at this moment his cousin would be travelling directly to a much warmer place.

"Pray remember you are on MacIntyre land and speak to its laird."

Red bowed mockingly. "Aye, madam. As neither of you will listen to reason about an alliance, I'll take my leave. Just remember, *Glennoe*, you can only hold the wolves at bay for so long."

"If an alliance is needed so badly by the MacDonalds," said Maude, her gaze icy, "perhaps you should find a wife."

"I'll be wed soon enough," said Red with a shrug. "I have my eye on a great prize in Stirling, and travel tomorrow to win it. Farewell."

When his cousin's heavy footsteps were no more than a faint tap on the stairs below, Callum sighed and slumped into a chair beside the library fireplace. "Do not say a word, Mother."

"Who, me?" she replied archly, adding a piece of wood to the fire before stepping back and smoothing her cream velvet gown. With her pale skin and long fair hair, those violet eyes were even more startling. His father had seen her at an English tourney and been so captivated by her ethereal beauty he'd brought her home. Callum arrived nine months later, but no other children followed. Knowing how miserable the marriage had been, he could easily understand why she didn't seek another husband. In time perhaps she might seek a lover, and he would support her happiness wholeheartedly.

"Yes, you."

"I only speak up because Rory grows in confidence and supporters. Be wary, my son. Why would he travel to Stirling?"

Callum frowned. "I don't know. It is a long distance for someone who always picks the lowest hanging fruit. And if he had an audience with the king, he would brag of it."

"Exactly. Let us hope dear Alastair brings news when he returns from the market."

He looked away, so his mother might not see his true heart. It was getting harder and harder to conceal his feelings for Alastair Graham. Twenty years prior, Maude had rescued a starving, sickly boy abandoned by a roving clan. Once Alastair had healed, Callum had begged for him to be allowed to stay. They had become close friends, and after years of playing, exploring, and studying, Alastair was appointed his official squire. Eventually they fought and drank and wenched together, although sometimes Alastair bedded men instead. Callum had never quite known how to feel about that. The clergy said lust between men was wrong, but Alastair held no shame or guilt about it, and sometimes the need that coursed through Callum's veins when he thought about his squire shocked him. As the laird's heir, he could do nothing about it, and they had remained just the best of friends.

Until the night Callum's father was buried.

Overwhelmed with regret at things unsaid and the heavy burden now on his unworthy shoulders, Callum had paced his bedchamber for hours. Yet when Alastair's awkward words and soothing massage turned into intoxicating kisses, Callum had discarded all good sense and pleaded to be taken so he might forget his cares for a little while. His squire had been tender and gentle to start, then rough and demanding with mouth and hands and cock, leaving Callum sore and so thoroughly pleasure-sated he'd actually slept with a measure of peace in his soul. But as the first rays of dawn inched their way through the tapestries, he made the hardest and worst decision of his life: telling his lover of one night that it could never happen again. That they must never speak of it. And they hadn't.

Except he couldn't forget.

Now he knew the firmness of Alastair's lips, those huge callused hands that could grip like a vise or stroke like a butterfly wing, the sweet burn of thick cock inside him, no other would do. Rather confusing for a man who desired women and enjoyed the taste and silken clasp of wet cunt; terribly unhelpful for a laird who needed to wed and sire an heir. He did not have the luxury of following his heart; certainly not to love a penniless squire. His future was naught but cold duty, for the only way to save his people and lands was to wed a Highland heiress from a clan powerful enough that the Campbells would never encroach again.

But what grand lady would marry an unimportant laird in an isolated glen?

"Good afternoon, laird. Lady Maude."

The familiar low, rasping voice jolted Callum from his thoughts, and he turned to see Alastair enter the room. God's blood, he was handsome. Everything about his squire roared dominant rebellion; untamable shoulder-length brown hair, piercing blue eyes, and a build so tall and brawny it was forever threatening to destroy the clothing that encased it. Several noble houses had offered Alastair good coin to be a bodyguard, and while he'd refused them all so far, even the thought of losing him was terrifying.

"Dear boy," said Maude fondly, stepping forward to smooth a lock of Alastair's windswept hair, as she'd done since they were children. An act he'd always longed to do, but never dared.

Instead, Callum took a deep breath to quell his arousal and relief at Alastair's nearness, and smiled in greeting. "What news from the market? Red just informed us he travels to Stirling on the morrow to win some prize. Mother and I hoped you might know more, for he would not say."

His closest friend did not smile in return. In fact, he looked pained.

"You must travel too, Callum."

"What? Why?"

Alastair folded his massive arms. "Red goes to take part in the royal tourney that was just announced. All unwed men ranked knight, lord, or laird may enter, with a squire to assist."

"A *tourney*?" said Maude, her eyes gleaming with curiosity. "James has not held one in a long time. A boon for the queen?"

"Nay, to decide the husband of a wayward noblewoman. The lady suggested it herself; the prize is her hand in marriage, substantial dowry...and the friendship of her clan."

"Who is the lass?" asked Callum abruptly. "Which clan?"

Alastair hesitated; his blue eyes stormy with an unnamable emotion. "Lady Isla Sutherland."

The last Sutherland heiress!

His shoulders fell. Marriage to Lady Isla would solve all his woes, but he may as well wish to conquer the sky. Men would come from all corners of Scotland to compete for such a treasure. Skilled, athletic warriors, worthy of her hand.

Devil take it. A failure he would remain.

And his clan would be slowly destroyed.

๑๕๑

After twenty-eight summers on this earth, he'd learned one thing: those he loved were destined never to love him in return. His mother and father. His clan.

Callum.

Alastair Graham leaned against the cool stone wall, just to keep distance between himself and his laird. Any closer and he would be tempted to gaze into those near-silver eyes that reminded him of spring rain, stroke his hair, and listen to his cares so he might thrash whoever had displeased or harmed him. But Callum didn't want that; he'd made his thoughts quite plain after their unforgettable night together. Since then, a fierce battle raged within Alastair each day: to stay and endure this half-life or leave to no life at all. He always remained. Never would he abandon his laird, not when he needed him so much. But plague take it, this choice was difficult to bear.

If he had any regrets, it was that one night. Protecting his laird, assisting him each day would be so much easier if he didn't know the heaven of hot kisses, the sweet sound of Callum's pleasured moans, the feverish ride to release followed by the peace of embracing until dawn. Since his banishment from Callum's bed he'd been in a terrible state, desperately needing the release of a good fuck and yet unwilling to take another, lass or lad. He couldn't. Not after having Callum.

Sometimes he wondered if Lady Maude guessed that the friendship between her only child and the lad she'd fostered had gone further. She never said a word about it; yet the clan healer saw far deeper into the souls of men than they liked or wished. Those fathomless violet eyes missed nothing.

"Callum," said Alastair eventually, when the silence in the cozy library stretched too long. "You must try for Lady Isla's hand in the tourney. Not just for the dowry and a friendship with the Sutherlands, but the lass herself. She's bold and strong and would give you fine children."

The words actually hurt to say. But he had to set aside the frustration and jealousy at the thought of Callum with another, for the clan that had saved his life and given him the only home he'd ever known, were in the worst kind of trouble. He would do whatever it took to ensure the survival of the MacIntyres, even if that meant losing the man he loved forever.

His laird sighed. "I fear it would be a wasted journey. What chance would I have?"

"Every chance," he said too-fiercely.

Lady Maude glanced his way, but merely nodded. "Listen to Alastair, my son. It won't be one of the English tourneys that your father so loved. James is a modern king. A scholar, much like yourself. He won't risk death or serious injury to the most important men in his realm, it will be a tourney in name only, an occasion for pageantry and color to show all comers that Scotland is not inferior, but a great kingdom."

"You think?" said Callum, looking unconvinced.

"Aye. James uses force when given no choice, but at heart he is a gallant. Lady Isla could not have suggested a more pleasing idea, for in the guise of granting her a boon, he helps himself far more. You and Alastair must go. I beg you."

Silence again filled the library, and when Alastair sent Callum a pointed glance, the younger man sighed and held up his hands in surrender. Many would hear Maude's words as no more than a motherly lecture, but they knew better. She'd *seen* something in the mist of her mind. It didn't happen often, but her words always came to pass. He had more reason than most to be grateful for the gift; it was the reason he'd been found all those years ago and brought back here to the castle.

"Very well," said Callum. "But what of you, Mother?"

"I shall remain here and guard your lands, of course," said Maude in a lofty tone that suggested it had been a foolish question.

Alastair almost smiled. The Lady of Glennoe might be English, but she was as bold and brave as any Highland woman. If Lady Isla was of similar character—as she'd been caught disguised as a lad and sword fighting, he couldn't believe otherwise—then a laird with complementary traits like an even temper, kind heart, and scholarly mind, might make a favorable impression at least. But success would all depend on what the tourney events were.

"There'll be men at arms to assist you, lady," he said, more to ease Callum's anxiety. Despite a fractured relationship with his father, he'd been grief-stricken at his death. But to lose his beloved mother as well...that, Callum would not recover from.

"I shall go and advise them now," said Maude, dipping into a curtsy. "Do not forget to take your satchel of herbs, salves, and poultices to Stirling, my son. On the morrow, I shall bless your journey and bid you both farewell with a glad heart. Good day to you. And you, Alastair."

After she departed, Callum walked across the library to his favorite 'thinking' window. As he'd discarded his mantle in the warmth of the fire-heated room and wore only an embroidered doublet and hose, his unhurried gait offered prime viewing of his perfect arse.

"A tourney in Stirling to try and win a rich wife," Callum

said, absently tracing a pattern in the cool stone with his elegant fingers. "Not how I foresaw my next few weeks."

Alastair moved closer, attracted like a moth to flame. "Leave such gifts to your lady mother. She is never wrong."

His laird nodded. "She did bring you home, after all. And also assumed you would travel with me to Stirling. But I shall ask. Will you be at my side for the tourney?"

At your side? Always.

"Yes," he rasped, placing one paw of a hand on his laird's narrow shoulder. "Callum—"

The younger man inhaled unsteadily. "I feel all at sea not even knowing what events I must take part in, and there'll be men twice my size from all over Scotland eager to humiliate me on the field. After that, if by some miracle I win, my reward is wedding a stranger."

Unbidden, Alastair's other hand rose to rest on Callum's shoulder, and he kneaded the rigid muscles. Once upon a time his laird had welcomed regular massages; he had an unfortunate habit of sitting hunched over documents and manuscripts until his back seized up. But since that night, touch had become too much of a temptation, and Alastair rarely allowed himself the pleasure. "We'll take each day as it comes. But I will need to work on these slabs of stone—"

"They are. I miss your massages," said Callum softly.

Alastair gritted his teeth. He missed giving them, for he preferred touch to words in demonstrating care. But for his own peace of mind, he couldn't torture himself like that. "Well. You'll need one after each event, or you'll be too stiff the following day."

"Each event? Now that is confidence, presuming I will succeed. Far more likely I'll be one of the unfortunates riding away in the dead of night after being soundly defeated in the first round."

"Continue thinking like that, and you will be," said Alastair irritably, hating that Callum thought so little of his own abilities thanks to the long shadow of his late father. "I doubt all events will reward brute strength. Some perhaps, but we know the king also values intellect and strategy. Besides, you really think all those trying for Lady Isla's hand will be part mountain? Not everyone in the realm is Sir Lachlan Ross."

"Or you," said Callum, tilting his head back to look up, his cheeks pink.

Plague take it, he loved that blush. Callum was too-often bound by harsh reality, but his sweet soul always found a way to shine through. Yet another reason he craved his laird so helplessly.

Alastair cleared his throat. "Speaking of Sir Lachlan, he is to be the chief judge, so at least the contests will be fair. He would never permit trickery...well, apart from letting a lass dress as a lad to learn sword fighting from him."

"*What?*"

"I should have said earlier. That is the reason for the tourney; Isla told her father and mother she traveled to St. Andrews to learn piety, instead she disguised herself as a lad for months and attended Sir Lachlan's trainings. I hear she is uncommonly good with sword in hand; but she is not permitted to fight any longer. Poor lass. Imagine having great skill at something and being forbidden from doing it..."

Like bedding my laird.

"Anyway," Alastair continued, "There'll be a feast at Stirling Castle on Sunday to announce the five events and introduce all the lords, lairds, and knights. Then one event each day where men will either progress or retire, before Lady Isla weds the winner."

Callum nodded thoughtfully. "I've never met a lady sword fighter. She does sound interesting."

Jealousy flared again.

It was a terrible thing and quite unworthy of their longtime friendship, that he wished for victory to gain the money and alliance, but defeat so he would not lose Callum forever.

Alas, he suspected that Lady Isla Sutherland might just turn their entire existence upside down. For a man who spent every day striving to earn his place at Glennoe, an unnerving thought indeed.

CHAPTER 2

Stirling

The number of people gathering in anticipation of the tourney was staggering.

From the relative safety of the modest but comfortable two-roomed cottage provided by a distant cousin of his father's, Callum watched the frantic activity down in the village proper. It seemed half of Scotland had arrived already; musicians, tinkers, blacksmiths, and pie sellers all jostling for space with lasses offering everything from mending to healing elixirs to a quick fuck. Indeed, anything could be purchased...apart from lodgings, as increasingly angry travelers with overstuffed luggage wagons were discovering.

He shook his head. There was as much chance of finding rooms in Stirling now as the kings of England and France swearing fealty to James. This cottage was perfectly placed though; probably no more than a few hundred yards to the castle gates, and next door there was a stall for the horses, generous supply of hay, and a small well for water. They'd also secured the services of a young lad to feed and walk them each day. Inside the cottage boasted a well-stocked larder, even proper beds with straw mattresses and thick quilts rather than wooden pallets. He and Alastair had been fortunate to get so close; Stirling Castle was unusual in that it had few rooms for guests. What it did have was the largest and most magnificent Great Hall in Scotland, a newly-finished, lime-washed structure that shone like gold and could be seen from miles around. It was there they would meet Lady Isla today, before the tourney began in the morning.

"Shall we go and register, then?"

At Alastair's voice in his ear, Callum near-trembled. The long ride to Stirling had been punishing, he'd insisted on short rests so they might have a few days here before the tourney started. But staying here together in a private dwelling with thick stone walls, all he could think about was that night in his bedchamber when his closest friend had owned him body and soul.

How long could he choose duty when faced with such overwhelming temptation?

"Yes, we should register. Far more chance of winning a bride if I'm on the lists," he jested weakly.

"You look well. Prosperous."

Callum glanced down at his dark brown hose, fine linen shirt embroidered at the cuffs and neck with sprigs of heather, blue velvet doublet, and black cloak. It was true, even if he lacked the size of a warrior or the wealth of a grand lord, at least he looked the part of a laird. Before the latest raid, the garments created in his weaving house had been the finest in Scotland; the clan especially noted for quality hose and stockings. His coffers might be nearly empty, but the wooden closets, chests, and drawers were full. "Aye. The false-hoods fine clothing can tell."

Alastair snorted. "There'll be many men hiding empty purses behind clothes and jewels this week. You think they all came to Stirling to win Lady Isla for her wit or fair face?"

"God's blood, I felt the scolding lash of that eyebrow raise from here. I surrender the point."

"Only the point, alas."

Yearning nearly crushed him. Nothing would raise his spirits and calm his nerves more than pleasure. Those sturdy beds were right there...

Swallowing hard, Callum straightened his shoulders. "We must go."

While it was a short walk to the castle, the path grew much steeper as they neared the imposing gray stone structure perched atop Castle Hill. It offered a breathtaking view of the surrounding lands, and in the distance the River Forth twisted and turned in several directions, like a lady's hair ribbon dropped on the ground. Several burly men at arms guarded the gates, and when he and Alastair approached, one stepped forward.

"Good morrow. State your name and purpose, sirs."

"Good morrow," said Callum, holding out his right hand to show he held no weapon and came in peace, and also to display his hereditary gold ring with the clan crest stamped upon it. "I am Callum MacIntyre, clan chief and Lord of Glennoe, here to register for the king's tourney. This is my squire, Master Alastair Graham."

"Welcome," said the man, inclining his head. "The king is in the Great Hall, but you must first register in the outer close. We are all eager to watch the events. Good fortune to you."

"My thanks."

There was something special about Stirling Castle. While

the Great Hall and the forework with its towering gatehouse and conical roofs were new, there were parts of the castle that were hundreds of years old. It had withstood siege and war, not to mention many changes of ownership between Scot and Englishman. The tales those thick stone walls could tell!

Alastair cleared his throat, giving him a look that said he'd tarried too long. Cheeks heating, Callum entered the short, dark tunnel under the forework, before emerging in the wide empty space of the cobblestoned outer close.

Struck speechless, he could only stare in awe at the massive Great Hall in front of him. After the darkness of the tunnel, the limewashed stone gleamed like heaven itself.

"Glennoe!"

At the unexpected hail he turned to see the King of Scotland approaching, black velvet mantle fluttering in the light breeze, and the heavy chain of state clinking about his neck. How on earth did James remember him? They'd only met twice; the last time several years ago at a meeting of Highland lairds.

"Your Grace!" Callum replied, as he and Alastair dropped to one knee before kissing the gold ring on the king's outstretched hand, a renewed pledge of loyalty to the crown.

"I'm pleased you are entering my tourney," continued James in excellent Gaelic. "You and Master Graham are most welcome to Stirling Castle. My condolences on the loss of your father, but I hear great progress has been made in talks and trade. Sometimes a warrior is needed. Sometimes a gentler touch, eh?"

The king was *extremely* well-informed.

Stunned, Callum rose to his feet. "Thank you, Your Grace. I was just admiring the buildings. Old and new together."

James beamed. "As it should be. Honor the past, welcome the future. 'Tis the only way to secure Scotland's place in the world. Now. Go and register, then come into the Hall. I shall be announcing the five events very soon."

Still reeling from his audience with their sovereign, brief though it was, it took a nudge from Alastair to get him moving to the trestle table where two stern faced men clad in black robes stood. Ugh. *Lawyers.* "Good morrow, sirs. I am Callum MacIntyre, clan chief and Lord of Glennoe. This is my squire, Master Alastair Graham."

"Good morrow. Write your name here," said one of the men briskly, pointing to an empty line near the bottom of a large piece of parchment. Gah. So many names already, including his wretched cousin.

"Very well."

"Then make your mark in the red wax with your crest. His Grace takes no responsibility for injury or death resulting from this tourney. Do you understand and consent?"

"I do," said Callum, only his mother's reassurance about the probable events suppressing an involuntary shudder at the ominous words.

The lawyer added a drop of wax to the parchment, and Callum pressed his ring into it. There. He was officially on the lists.

"You're doing the right thing," said Alastair as they walked to the Great Hall and ascended the front steps.

"Remind me of that on the morrow when I'm curled up in a corner..."

His words trailed off, for at the other end of the Hall on the dais reserved for royalty and honored guests, stood King James, Queen Margaret...and a captivating stranger.

Surely not Lady Isla?

Callum weaved his way through the growing crowd so he might get a closer look. The woman was similar in height to him, her slender form encased in a costly scarlet velvet gown with jeweled girdle and heavily embroidered sleeves. Hair as black as night peeked out from under her gable hood. She did not smile and her creamy skin held the pallor of someone uncomfortable in their surroundings, but her emerald eyes near gleamed with defiance and fierce intelligence.

When her gaze settled on him, he caught his breath at the jolt of awareness that passed through his body.

Then she winked.

Startled, he laughed, and when she smiled in return, one full of mischief and barely leashed sensuality, he blushed like a virgin.

Alastair elbowed him and Callum winced at the gouge to his ribs, while appreciating the reminder to behave like a gallant and not a simpering fool. But his attraction to the lady was entirely unexpected. If his heart had long ago settled on Alastair, why did he now feel like it could expand and make room for her as well?

Troubled, Callum looked away. How typical to be having such thoughts when there were countless obstacles in his path. Namely the thirty or so knights, lords, and lairds in this Hall who would fight to the death for a prize like Lady Isla Sutherland.

The chance of him winning her hand was very small indeed.

⚜

Who were they?

Isla forced herself to remain on the dais with the king and queen, rather than leaping into the fray of men to meet the two who had caught her attention.

One was of average height, beautifully dressed, fair-haired, possessing a merry grin and an air of such gentle sweetness that she was torn between wanting to hold him close and corrupting him with the naughtiest behavior she could think of. The other was a tall, brawny, brown-haired man in plain but well-made clothing, who gazed at her with cool sternness. Not dislike, just wary caution. The way he stood half a step behind the other man, his eyes darting about and assessing potential threats reminded her greatly of Sir Lachlan's protectiveness toward his wife and mistress, which made him even more interesting.

She wanted to talk to both of them at once. Discover their names, their character, their reason for entering the tourney.

Kiss them.

Isla blinked at the startling thought. Apart from worshipping Sir Lachlan, she'd never really been tempted by the men —young or old—around her. The goal of returning to her clan in triumph as a warrior had been all-consuming; only improving her sword fighting had mattered. Besides, no fine arse, large cock bulge, or broad shoulders could compare to the heady thrill of victory. It was a glorious moment indeed when all the failures, the aching limbs and blisters and cuts, the will to be better and faster and more skilled, resulted in a conquered opponent.

Yet these men, she wanted. And not one or the other, but *both*. Her former sword master kissed two women. Why could she not kiss two men?

"Lady Isla?"

She forced her gaze away from the strangers, to look at the king. "Your Grace?"

"We shall begin. I'll introduce you, then draw the tourney events from the sack held by Queen Margaret. If you would read aloud each card to confirm the event and order, I would be most obliged."

"Of course," she said, as her palms grew damp. No turning back now.

James clapped his hands together twice, and a hush

descended on the Great Hall. "My queen. Lords, lairds, and knights. Honored guests. I am delighted to introduce Lady Isla, youngest daughter of the Earl and Countess of Sutherland. As you can see, she is a true Highland lass of beauty and spirit who will make the tourney winner a splendid wife. Now it is time to announce the events. As this is Scotland, they shall be activities popular in this realm and no other. There will not be a joust."

Murmurs echoed in the Hall; some men looked disappointed while others were relieved. In truth Isla shared that relief; many years ago an older cousin had died after an opponent's lance found a gap in his armor and pierced his flesh. The wound had putrefied, poisoning his blood, and she would not wish that slow and agonizing passing on anyone.

"And so," the king continued, "let us discover the first event to be held on the morrow. My queen?"

Margaret, elegantly clad in pale blue velvet, gold girdle, and jeweled gable hood, smiled and held up a small black satin sack. He rummaged inside and pulled out a card, then gave it to Isla to read.

She took a deep breath. "The first event is...a foot race! There shall be six races, each with five men competing over a half-mile distance. The first three men in each race shall progress. All others must retire from the tourney."

The murmurs rose to a low roar, and Isla stifled a smile at the shocked dismay on certain faces. She was pleased to note that her fair-haired favorite and his squire had brightened at the news.

In quick succession, the king handed her three more cards to read, each event progressing men or sending them home. The second day would be archery, the third a heaving of the stone put, the fourth an occasion of revels; music and dancing. Even from her place on the dais she could see frowns and glares and gritted teeth at the choices the king had made, but if the entrants were surprised, they did not know their sovereign at all. James was a modern king and expected others to follow his enlightened lead.

As each event was called her favorite relaxed further, even grinning at his squire, and her heart leaped. One more. All they needed was one more event he might excel at, and there was a chance she could wed a man she very much liked the look of.

The king paused until the Hall became silent again, allowing the tension to build before handing her the fifth parchment card.

Isla beamed. "The final event shall be...sword fighting! It is anticipated four men shall remain on the last day, so there will be preliminary fights in the morning and a final fight for the two victors in the afternoon. The grand winner of the tourney shall gain my hand in marriage, my dowry, the friendship of the Sutherlands, and a gift of cloth from the royal household."

Cheers echoed loudly, the din almost deafening, and Isla curtsied. While her head remained modestly bowed, she allowed her gaze to flick up to the two men in the audience, eager to see their reaction to the final event that would win her hand.

They weren't smiling now. In fact, both looked grim.

Her heart plummeted. What on earth was the matter? Every knight, lord, and laird could fight with a sword; they were taught as lads, and with Scotland being Scotland, had ample opportunity to hone such a skill throughout their life.

James called for silence once more. "A final warning. This tourney will be judged by me, and my champion, Sir Lachlan Ross, who will cast a very stern eye over proceedings. Apart from a squire, or healer in the event of injury, entrants are permitted no other assistance. Deception, evil deeds, or other mischief will not be tolerated. Anyone committing such acts shall be banished in disgrace or even imprisoned. I will have an honorable husband for this lady, not a scoundrel. Now. My lawyer shall read out all the names, and each entrant may make himself known to Lady Isla."

The long line of men soon became a blur, and she couldn't even say if she nodded or smiled or even replied to those who bowed and kissed her hand. The only two she wanted to meet were her fair-haired favorite and his brawny friend; especially to inquire why they'd looked so unhappy at being asked to sword fight.

Naturally, they were the very last names on the list.

An hour later, with the Hall empty apart from the king and queen who were warming their hands in front of one of the five fireplaces, Isla finally stood alone with the two she wished to. This close they were even more handsome, and her mind waged a war against her body; the desire to know everything about them against the desire to stroke and caress.

Hurling good manners out the window, Isla looked impatiently at both. "Your names again, sirs? Why did you look so miserable at the thought of swords?"

The fair-haired man bowed over her hand. Intriguingly, his eyes were almost silver. "I am Callum MacIntyre, clan chief and Lord of Glennoe. From the Western Highlands, on the shores of Loch Etive, my lady. This is my squire and close friend, Master Alastair Graham."

The brawny, brown-haired man inclined his head, his watchful eyes as blue as a summer sky. "Lady."

Her whole body tingled with excitement. What was it about these two that interested her so? They weren't the most important men in the tourney, nor the wealthiest, or in possession of the most land. "You looked pleased at the events until the last. Why is that? You're a Highland laird, Glennoe!"

Those beautiful gray eyes met hers for the longest

moment, as though he might see into her soul, then he shrugged. "In truth, my lady, while my late father was a renowned swordsman, I am his gravest disappointment: a scholar. Aye, I can run, shoot an arrow, dance and play a tune, maybe even heave a stone a little distance. But I've never been skilled with a sword and Alastair fights best with fists or dagger. I fear that, even if by some miracle I made it to the last event, I would be soundly defeated."

Isla wanted to howl in dismay. This laird had answered her honestly, but what comfort could she offer? He spoke the truth. There was no way a poor swordsman would win the tourney.

Unless...

What if she disobeyed the king's rules and offered training in secret? Next to Sir Lachlan, no other could better assist Glennoe. Yes, honorable reluctance would be understandable, but if they were intrigued by her enough to risk it, if they would accept a woman's guidance...

All she could do was wait for a pause in conversation, then casually make an offer. The next step would be up to them.

⚜

He'd not thought this situation could get any more complicated than being in love with Callum, and half-supporting, half-loathing his quest for a wealthy bride to secure the clan's future.

He was wrong.

Alastair observed in silence as his laird and Lady Isla continued a frank discussion about swords. There was a spark of mutual interest and awareness between them that made his heart clench. But far worse...he wanted this rebellious lady swordfighter, this beauty with flashing green eyes, black curls to tangle his fingers in, and small breasts to close his mouth around. In his bed, bent over a desk, braced against a wall... begging him to fuck her harder, for she would be no shy lass in her needs.

But he couldn't have her. Either he and Callum would return to Glennoe with nothing to show for the journey and expense, or his laird would have a new bride belonging to him alone. Then his existence would be the torture of watching the man he loved with a woman he desired; forever excluded by the little intimacies of marriage, the glances and smiles, casual touches and private conversations. Forever aware that at night Callum would use that willing tongue, eager hands, and unflagging cock to ensure a happy wife.

Once again, he would be alone.

"I know you have a special gift with swords, Lady Isla," said Alastair abruptly, ashamed at his irritable, bitter tone yet unable to halt it. "But why do you care if my laird does not?"

She looked at him with those wide emerald eyes, but rather than flaring with affront or anger, her gaze was thoughtful. "For one reason," she replied, her voice hushed so it didn't carry to royal ears. "I should like to help."

"*Why?*" he repeated, folding his arms and pinning her with a glare.

Lady Isla raised an eyebrow, utterly unbothered by the stance, and his admiration for her unwillingly grew. "I suspect, Master Graham, for the same reason you are so protective. I like him."

Callum's indrawn breath echoed in the cavernous expanse of the empty Hall, and Alastair coughed to ensure the king and queen did not grow suspicious and join them in conversation. They probably had only a few moments more to talk, then the lady would be escorted back to her family or maybe a private gathering for high-ranking courtiers.

"How do you mean...help?" whispered Callum, his brow

furrowing a little. "The king specifically forbids it in the tourney rules."

Lady Isla cast a furtive glance at James and Margaret before straightening her shoulders. "You told me a truth of yours, allow me to return the favor. I would have been content to continue my lessons with Sir Lachlan, to one day fight for my clan or Scotland, even act as an envoy for the king. I never sought a husband, and only suggested this tourney to delay a forced marriage to a rotten apple whom I would never love, and would never love me."

Alastair nodded in reluctant sympathy. Wealth smoothed away many cares, but it was men who gained. Daughters of great houses were seen as tools to advance the family, not as people deserving of love or happiness. Women of humble birth might have few material comforts, but when it came to choosing a husband or lover, they had much greater freedom. "The lot of a noblewoman."

"Indeed. But then I saw Glennoe. He laughed at my wink, blushed at my regard, answered my question honestly, and you are loyal unto him in a way that commends his character. That makes me think there is a chance for me to have a happy future."

A glance across the Hall confirmed that the king watched them even as he laughed at something his young queen said. But curiously, he remained beside the fireplace. Did James approve of Callum as a suitor? Or did he have devious motives yet to be revealed?

Alastair gripped his arms so tightly he left imprints on his skin. "And so, lady?"

"Glennoe states he can run, shoot an arrow, dance, play a tune, and heave a stone a little. Thus, an even chance of progressing through the early events—"

"More than even," he growled. "My laird is a man of many talents."

"*Alastair*," chided Callum, but his gaze was warm.

"Forgive me," he said stiffly. "I mean no offense."

Lady Isla tilted her head. "I know you don't. I'd wager Glennoe has far more talents than many would guess, and is far too modest to list them. However, he confesses a weakness in his ability with a sword. One talent I will never hide, nor be modest about, is swordplay. I was Sir Lachlan's best student until my tumble from grace. What I am offering is... lessons. In secret. If you wish, Glennoe. If marriage to me, knowing how unconventional I am, might be something you truly desire."

Sword lessons!

Alastair met Callum's troubled gaze, knowing he would be torn at such an offer. Honor demanded they obey the king's rules; yet both knew if Callum did manage to reach the last four, with his current ability he would have no chance in winning the tourney. The other entrants had fought in vicious clan battles, committed daring border raids against the English, and stood shoulder to shoulder with the king as he quelled uprisings. Thanks to years of cruelty; the mockery and beatings that had followed each defeat by his father, other clan members, or his cousin, Callum hated to even pick up a sword. But with Lady Isla as a tutor, maybe he could learn some new skills or improve his stance and grip and footwork just enough to hold his own against the other men.

Alas, they had no more time to discuss the matter, for the king and queen now approached.

"The minutes have flown in the company of a fine lass," Alastair said too-heartily, bowing to Lady Isla. "Laird, we should go and begin preparations for the foot race on the morrow. The competition shall be fierce."

Lady Isla held out her hand to Callum. "It was a great pleasure to meet you, Glennoe. I look forward to hearing your opinion on a great Highland pastime. Good fortune to you and your squire in the tourney."

Callum bowed over her hand, then rather daringly for him, kissed it. "Thank you, my lady. I hope—"

"Isla!" said Margaret as she joined them. "Your father and mother eagerly await you. Do not tarry in this Hall any longer."

The lady didn't express annoyance at her fourteen-year-old queen's scolding by even a glance or twitch, yet somehow Alastair could feel it and he admired the restraint. He felt much sympathy for the king and the sacrifices he'd made to ensure the unholy alliance with England succeeded. Everyone in the realm knew James didn't love his Tudor wife, but he was always courteous, and to placate her further, he'd sent his mistresses and all the illegitimate children he doted on far away from Stirling Castle.

"Yes, Your Grace," Lady Isla said, curtsying deeply. "Good day, all."

The king smiled as he watched her leave the Great Hall. "A great treasure for the worthy winner of my tourney. Are you pleased with the five events, Glennoe?"

Alastair tensed at the seemingly innocent question. He remained wary of their sovereign's indulgence of time just now, and what purpose that might serve. For James would certainly have a purpose. Their king might be younger and far more amiable than most, but he had already proven himself a formidable, shrewd, and practical man. Much like Callum, James was forced each day to mend the mistakes of his father as best he could.

Callum inclined his head. "They honor the character of my king perfectly, I believe. Part warrior, part gallant. So yes, Your Grace, I shall be pleased to demonstrate a range of skills in the quest to win the hand and heart of Lady Isla. And to provide a spectacle for the enjoyment of my queen."

"Well said, well said," murmured the king. "I expect great things from you, perhaps more so because you will not be expected to progress far. Prepare your laird well, Master Graham."

"Aye, Your Grace," he replied, understanding the dismissal for what it was.

Lest anything they said be overheard and repeated to spiteful ears, Alastair and Callum departed the Great Hall in silence, and held their tongues crossing the outer close also. Several of the other entrants remained outside, clearly hoping for further time with Lady Isla, or even a private audience with the king. From the expressions on their faces, they were furious that such a lowly laird had been permitted both—none more so than wretched Red MacDonald, who gave them both a dagger glare.

"Well," said Callum eventually, as they descended the steep path toward the cottage. "That was interesting. I have much to think about this evening."

Ha. Interesting was a woefully inadequate word for an afternoon where they'd met a bold, beautiful woman who offered the world...if they broke the rules. But his laird preferred to mull matters over before making a judgment, so there was no hurrying the conversation.

Tomorrow, however, would be a different tale entirely.

CHAPTER 3

I sla sat up in bed with a start, her heart pounding and limbs trembling.

For a moment she wondered if she'd cried out, but all around her was quiet, her father and mother still fast asleep on the other side of the chamber. After untangling the linen sheet and quilt from around her legs, she lay back on her pillow and let her eyes adjust to the faint flicker of smoldering fireplace and candle stubs in the pre-dawn gloom.

That dream.

Her cheeks flushed. She was no green girl; a virgin yes, but she'd seen and heard things that a youngest child tended to see and hear because others forgot she was there. Not to mention the ribald conversations and cock-waving jests made by the lads during rest times at St. Andrews. Yet her mind had taken that knowledge, Glennoe's kiss to her hand that had jolted her fair to her toes, and Master Graham's gruff questions and brawny folded arms, and blended it into something wickedly erotic.

She'd been naked, the men fully clothed. They had held her wrists behind her back while teasing her nipples to hard points, kissing her neck and lips before parting the bush of black hair that covered her mound, and caressing the tender pink pearl nestled there. As she'd whimpered and writhed at the sensual torment, each had taken one of her hands and guided it to their hose-covered cocks, telling her in blunt, raw terms what she must do to please them.

Naturally, that was the moment she'd woken. And now she needed to touch herself more than anything in the world, to ease the restless, pulsing ache at her center, something she usually only did after victory in a swordfight when her whole body burned with wild elation. In the past there had been a forbidden element to her pleasure, for in the absence of a man who heated her blood, it had been the thought of Sir Lachlan returning to the manor and bedding Lady Marjorie and Lady Janet that had brought her release. Now, all she could think of was Glennoe and Master Graham tearing away her shift and nightgown, roughly parting her thighs and holding them wide open as they explored the slick folds of her cunt.

"Yes," she whispered, turning onto her front before sliding a hand down between her legs to coat her fingertips in honey and rub her swollen pearl. "Please."

Hot tingles danced along her skin, as in her mind, the men each eased a finger into her tight channel. When she did the same, thrusting two fingers to the first knuckle, in and out and in and out, Isla had to muffle her gasp of release into the pillow.

Saints alive.

Flopping onto her back, she fought to catch her breath and not wake her father or mother. Thankfully no others shared their well-appointed chamber; their servants were in a small adjoining room. But even in here she dared not show a preference for Glennoe and his squire, let alone anywhere else in Stirling Castle or on the tourney field. The laird did not meet any of her family's requirements for a spouse. Sutherlands did not wed for love, kindness, interesting conversation or lust. They wed for wealth, land, and power. But she'd seen her fill of cold marriages, where the only thing that brought them satisfaction was destroying others.

She wanted warmth. Tender touch. The freedom to be her true self. So once again, her rebellious side had marched onward and she'd offered sword lessons in the hope that if Glennoe progressed to the final event of the tourney, he might win and take her to wife.

Would he accept her offer?

Isla burrowed under her quilt. Any decision to disobey the king needed time and much thought, but she hated not knowing Glennoe's mind.

Callum's mind.

Unwilling to say the names out loud, Isla wrote them instead across her quilt with a fingertip. *Callum MacIntyre, Lord of Glennoe. Isla MacIntyre, Lady of Glennoe, and her lover Master Alastair Graham.*

Heat scorched across her cheekbones. Somehow writing the forbidden wish was far more scandalous than what she'd imagined while touching herself. And yet already, her heart had decided this must be the way forward. All she had to do was convince Glennoe to accept her offer...

"Daughter! Get up. We'll be late for chapel."

Isla's eyes flew open at the sharp reprimand and she peered out from under the quilt. No. Her mother was wrong. Surely it couldn't be dawn. But weak rays of sunlight were beginning to lighten the chamber, which meant another endless day of formal court dress rather than the airy woolen hose and linen shirt that she'd worn while living and training at St. Andrews. Not a moment went by when she didn't think of those months of freedom; how she'd pretended to live with a noble family but instead rented a room from an elderly

widow nearby who feigned ignorance as long as three rules were followed: home by nightfall, coin paid each Sunday, and her ale left untouched.

All at once Isla's quilt was yanked away, and she yelped as the morning chill cooled her warm skin. "No need for that! I'm awake, Mother."

Lady Anne Sutherland glared at her, looking so elegant in her rose-pink velvet gown, gold girdle, and pearl-encrusted gable hood that Isla scowled. Her blue-eyed, fair-haired mother had been the celebrated beauty of her day, with marriage offers from across the realm and even England and France. It was decidedly unfair that her older sisters inherited that coloring while she resembled her father.

"Awake is not up, sponge-bathed, or dressed. Your sire has already departed to attend the king, I'll not have us late to chapel and be looked down upon by that puffed up child queen. I cannot believe James wed a Tudor; they've held the English throne all of five minutes. Any other royal bloodline would have been superior, even if the mother was a York. French, Spanish, Portuguese, even one of the Low Countries. It sticks in my craw to curtsy to her."

Familiar with this particular rant and well aware she was not required to reply, Isla merely nodded. In all honesty, she did not want to earn the queen's displeasure with a second scolding, not when she held such power by virtue of her position. Instead, Isla climbed out of bed, discarded her nightgown and shift, and hurried over to the washbasin to give herself a swift sponge bath. Thankfully, their longtime servant Morag had heated the water over the fire. "Which gown do you suggest I wear? To, ah, look nice."

And by look nice, I mean helpful in persuading Glennoe to accept sword lessons.

Anne blinked, her icy demeanor thawing a little. "The dark green will become you well, and the silver girdle to show off your narrow waist. A little padding to enhance your bodice—"

"No padding."

"When God is less then generous in his bounty, we must help ourselves."

"*No padding,*" Isla repeated. She would not pretend to have curves. Her body was her body, honed by countless hours of sweat-inducing sword fighting, and that was not something she would ever feel shame about.

Instead, she completed her sponging before Morag expertly dried her with a linen towel and assisted her into a fresh shift embroidered with roses at the neck.

Ugh. Dressing for court took forever.

Silk stockings affixed with garters. Linen kirtle. The dark green velvet gown with its square neckline, wide, fur-lined sleeves, low waist, and a train she found especially bothersome, for she often forgot it was there and dragged it through mud rather than hooking it up. Then the jewel-encrusted silver girdle around her waist. Lastly the tangles were combed from her unruly curls, and the cumbersome gable hood with a black velvet veil to cover her hair, was settled atop her head.

"Hmmm. You are too pale. No man wants a sickly-looking wife," said Anne, pinching her cheeks.

At last Isla was declared ready for chapel. Her stomach grumbled, but there was no point asking for bread and butter or small ale, there wasn't enough time.

"Will all the tourney entrants be at mass, do you think?" she asked carefully as they made their way from the chamber to the castle chapel at the edge of the inner close.

Anne nodded, her eyes gleaming. "If they are wise, they will be. I was pleasantly surprised at the quality of the men, considering you are the prize. Some great lords indeed. Enough land and position to ensure our clan remains high and mighty as we should and deserve to be. You have a favorite?"

"No, no," Isla replied quickly. "It's too soon. And so many men. I shall know better after the foot race, I think."

A lie, but under no circumstances would she reveal her preference. Knowing what her mother was capable of and how easily she could strike made Isla's stomach roil.

She wanted to help Glennoe and his squire, not hurt them.

He'd known it wouldn't take long for the games to begin—the jests, the pointed questions, the exclusion from gatherings of other entrants—but that 'noble' men could be so petty never failed to irritate him.

Alastair ground his teeth as weak rays of sunlight attempted to warm the cobblestoned inner close of Stirling Castle and Callum explained, once again, that he was a laird. Yes, he owned castle and lands. No, the members of his clan weren't cows, sheep, and rabbits. No, he didn't require a wooden block to stand on so he might be seen. And all the while, that hell-spawned Red MacDonald stood and smirked rather than offering even a hint of family loyalty.

His laird had the patience of a saint. If their positions were reversed, there would be a pile of high-ranking men at the foot of the cliffs surrounding the castle. And Red would be at the very bottom of that pile.

"Tell me, Glenbow, is it?" said one ruddy-cheeked border lord. "What are your thoughts on the foot race, this day? Not anxious that you'll be trampled, are you?"

Callum smiled. "Glennoe. I look forward to testing my skill against the other four men in my race."

"No doubt. Could be quite an advantage being so small and slight."

Red chuckled as he lounged against the steps of the Great Hall. "All those years being chased by chickens will finally bear fruit, cousin."

Raucous laughter echoed in the inner close, and it took several deep breaths for Alastair to contain his temper and not rearrange the collection of weak jaws. Earlier in the morning the noblemen had been on their best behavior in the cool, dark, incense-scented chapel, all devout and stately as though envoys of God himself. Then they'd turned into fawning flatterers as they'd greeted Lady Isla and her mother, praising everything but their toenails. The only gratifying moment had been the way Lady Isla's forced smile turned genuine when it rested on him and Callum. Ah, she was a beauty.

But out here in the large paved space between the King's House and the Great Hall, it seemed all gloves were off, and entrant's claws unleashed. He'd had quite enough and was ready to accept Lady Isla's offer on Callum's behalf no matter what objections he had. None of these pompous fools deserved a bold lady sword fighter at their side and sharing their bed.

"We shall see you on the field at noon," said Alastair shortly. "Good day to you all."

Callum inclined his head. "My lords. Sirs."

Somehow, he managed again to hold his tongue until they were on the path back to the cottage. "They may all go—"

"Wait for thick stone walls," said Callum. "Please."

By the time they were inside the cottage and had the door latched, Alastair's head was on the verge of explosion.

"Why?" he burst out. "Why do you let them speak to you like that? Especially Red? I know you prefer to be a peacemaker, but sometimes you must let loose that warrior inside you."

"Ah, Alastair," said his laird, sinking into a wooden chair, before pouring himself a goblet of wine, and downing it in a single gulp. "I think you may be the only soul on this earth apart from Mother who believes that I'm a warrior. Affection blindfolds you."

"You pay far too much heed to your father's words."

Callum frowned. "If I did possess a fighting spirit, I would be skilled with a sword. I'm not."

"So, you'll accept Lady Isla's help, then. Excellent."

"I have not made that decision as yet."

Alastair rubbed an impatient hand against his bearded jaw. How did he convince Callum of his worth when he judged his whole existence on what his late father had declared acceptable or nay? As often happened after an old laird passed, feats and victories were made greater, while weaknesses were set aside. Weaknesses like a hot temper, closed mind, or favoring a nephew over his own son because Red was taller and stronger and preferred fighting over learning.

But there was no point arguing. Not now, at least, when there was an event to prepare for. "Shall I bind your feet for the race?"

Callum smiled gratefully, although it was hard to know whether for the offer, or the change in subject. A subject they would return to, if Alastair had his way.

"Please. There are some linen bandages in my satchel, also a little clove oil to numb the soles of my feet. Then I won't feel it so much if they get cut or bruised. Fields can be traps for the unwary, no matter how green and welcoming they look."

"Clever," said Alastair, finding the items, then returning to kneel on the thick rug. "Give me your foot."

"There are many benefits in having a mother who is a healer," Callum replied as he removed his shoes and lower stockings and placed his right foot in Alastair's lap. "I find it reassuring that there are ways to ease all manner of ills, natural and unnatural."

His laird's foot was narrow and smooth yet quite large, and unable to halt himself, Alastair began with a gentle massage to warm the flesh. A low gasp made him raise his head to see Callum shudder and part his thighs a little. Emboldened, Alastair slid his hands up, rubbing the younger man's ankle, his calf, his knee, until Callum moaned.

"If I didn't know better," he murmured, "I might think you love this, that you crave my touch."

Callum swallowed hard. "It's just...it's just preparation. For the race."

"Is it? I'm reminded of that night I fucked you over and over, where I learned every inch of you with my fingers and tongue."

"*Alastair*. You swore never to speak of it again."

He leaned forward so his mouth was next to Callum's ear as his fingertips stroked the younger man's hose-clad inner thigh. To remind Callum who he truly belonged to, Alastair recklessly continued: "I wonder if you remember how it felt to have my cock in your mouth. In your arse. To be sticky with my seed and yours..."

Callum's finger's gripped his shirt, but eventually he pushed Alastair away. "Of course I remember," he said hoarsely. "Every single day. Never have I known such pleasure, or peace. But having you in my bed is a luxury I cannot afford. Only a wealthy bride and a strong alliance will save my clan. If by some miracle I won the tourney, do you think Lady Isla would wed me if she knew I sucked my squire's cock, that I'd begged him to fuck me harder? What do you think the Sutherlands would do?"

Alastair flinched. "The lady is unconventional. She might understand, even if her family disapproved..."

His words trailed off, for even he understood how foolish they were. Few wives would accept that their husband lusted after men as well as women. One of the reasons he'd not yet wed.

To distract himself from the harsh truth, Alastair took the small glass bottle of clove oil, shook some of the strong-smelling concoction onto a cloth, and dabbed it onto the underside of Callum's right foot. Then he did the same with the left. The skin went a little pink and blotchy, and having had this treatment before the removal of a splinter, he knew how odd and uncomfortable it felt. But as his laird had noted, it was far better than the alternative.

Once the oil had dried, he wrapped Callum's feet in a layer of linen bandage, under the arch and around the ankle, thick enough to provide some protection, but not so much it would impact mobility at all.

"There," he said at last. "Now you're ready to win a race and a bride. We should go to the field."

Callum took his hand and squeezed it. "Thank you. I know this is difficult. But without your support I have even less chance of success. That you are choosing to assist means the world to me. It is so very noble."

Alastair grunted. Maybe that would drown out the sound of his heart shattering into a thousand pieces. "After this morning, the less said about nobility, the better. If you don't leave those puffed-up peacocks—including your damned cousin—far behind, I'll thrash you myself."

"Aye, Master Graham."

The tender warmth in Callum's gaze hurt like the cauterizing of a wound. He would trade his soul for such looks every day, to be able to claim this man as his own, in bed and out, for the rest of his life. "Then let us march to the field of battle. At least in the foot race you must face just four other men, and defeat two, to proceed to the second event. After which you will make a decision on Lady Isla's offer. Swear that, at least."

His laird nodded slowly. "I do so swear."

Alastair repacked the satchel of salves, oils, concoctions, and bandages, but also added a small flagon of wine, and a cloth-wrapped parcel of dried fruit and chunks of soft white bread from the larder, as they would probably be hungry later.

But for now, Callum had a race to win.

Their very future depended on it.

☙❧

While the king hosted the tourney, the Sutherlands had funded it and spared no expense.

Callum halted, both impressed and overwhelmed. When he and Alastair first arrived in Stirling, this large field west of the castle had been a peaceful grazing spot for cows and sheep.

Now it was a battleground.

To their right, directly in front of the craggy cliffs and deep green vegetation of Castle Hill, sat the hastily constructed royal pavilion. Under the canopied roof were cushioned chairs for the king and queen, Lady Isla and the Sutherlands, honored guests like Lady Marjorie Ross and Lady Janet Fraser, privy councilors, and foreign envoys. Servants scurried about with trays of food and drink, as well as messages and documents for the king. Either side of the pavilion were long, tiered, wooden stands to accommodate wealthy spectators, and past those were large fenced areas where villagers crammed in to stand and watch. There were also refreshment stalls, and enterprising men and women walked about with trays selling small ale, meat pasties, and thick slices of fruit cake.

To their left was a long row of small white canvas tents, one for each tourney entrant. Outside each tent sat a sign with the entrant's clan badge painted upon it; about halfway down he could see the MacIntyre white heather. Well. That put a little spring in his step. Whoever arranged it had been exceedingly kind—each tent and sign were the same size, no matter the rank or wealth of the entrant. In this row at least, he belonged.

A trumpet blast sounded as he and Alastair took a knee in front of king and queen. For his own sanity, he did not look at Lady Isla.

"Son of the late Donald MacIntyre, Lord of Glennoe... presenting Callum MacIntyre, Lord of Glennoe. And his squire, Master Alastair Graham!"

At the herald's bellowed words, polite cheers rang out, and Callum raised his hand to acknowledge the crowd before he and Alastair walked to their tent.

"See?" said his squire. "The people want you to win."

"I doubt they have any idea who I am."

Alastair's brow furrowed. "You have distant kin in Stirling. Why should they not cheer you?"

"A truth," he conceded.

"You also assume that all other entrants are beloved. From the character demonstrated so far, I hardly believe that. If they treat you badly, how do you think they treat their tenants and servants? Strangers?"

Callum held up his hands, stifling a grin at the endearing irritability. "Very well, old man. Do not lose your voice lecturing me."

"Old man? I am three years your senior. And as vigorous and lusty as any here."

Another truth.

His bound feet had tingled after Alastair applied the numbing clove oil, but that sensation was nothing compared to the way his heart pounded and cock throbbed at the foot massage. He'd yearned then to not be laird, just a man who could indulge his desire for another man in the privacy of their own cottage. While his mind might try to forget, his needy body well remembered the rasp of Alastair's beard, the teasing lap of his tongue, and the brutal plunge of his huge cock.

A discreet cough jolted him from such ribald thoughts.

"Beg pardon, laird."

"Yes?" he replied, smiling at the guard wearing the king's livery and holding a large sack.

The man bowed. "In this sack are wooden squares painted six different colors. One color for each race, all those who select a blue square will race together and so forth. Each race will have five entrants; the first three will progress to the archery, the last two must retire from the tourney. Is that clear?"

"Indeed. Thank you."

"Choose your color, laird."

Callum delved into the sack and withdrew a square. "Green."

"Much obliged. Oh, green is the final race. Good fortune to you."

He groaned inwardly as the man made a note on his parchment before moving along to the next tent. Of course, it would be the final race, allowing him ample time to fret.

"Cousin," said Red, sauntering into the tent without invitation. "Bringing the MacIntyre name into disrepute already, I see. Are those *bandages* on your feet?"

"Good morrow," Callum replied stiffly. Red wore nothing but hose, his massive chest and shoulders glistening with oil, his feet bare. God's blood, he looked like a champion.

"Oh, you're in the green race. Shame. I hoped we might run against each other. I'm in the yellow race, which looks to be the most competitive."

"Shame indeed, Rory," said Alastair, clapping him hard on the shoulder.

Red glared at him, for he disliked his birth name. Then a sly smile lifted his lips. "I would stay, but I am invited to the royal pavilion to sit awhile with the Sutherlands. Lady Isla's request, I believe...safe travels back to Loch Etive, *Callum*."

His cousin actually whistled a cheery tune as he crossed the field to the pavilion, and Callum barely refrained from spitting in his general direction.

"Bah," said Alastair. "May his feet find every thistle and stone this field has to offer. I would give my last coin to see him fall on his face and finish last. Then we can wish him safe travels home."

Callum grinned reluctantly. "That would be most satisfying."

"Aye. Now, let's set this bench outside so we might watch the other races."

At first glance, the half-mile event seemed easy. Run the length of the field, around a flagpole raising the king's standard, then back. But as the first four races progressed in a blur of color, movement, and loud cheers, he saw athletic men falter. And each time, three men were jubilant, while two sank to their knees in despair, forced to leave the field.

Then came Red's race, the yellow group.

Callum prayed for a miracle: his cousin twisting an ankle, tripping over another, being overtaken at the finish. Naturally God ignored him, and that gleaming oiled chest led the race from start to end, to loud applause.

Plague take it, as his squire would say.

They made their way to the starting line, and Sir Lachlan

Ross stepped forward. "The last race! Green group, gather round."

Alastair gripped his shoulder. "You are an excellent runner, laird. Your feet are ready. Go well. I'll be waiting here to celebrate with you."

Callum took a deep breath, his stomach churning with anxiety. How did Alastair believe, when he did not? But he joined the line of four other men; an older knight from Edinburgh, two border lords, and a laird from somewhere near Inverness.

"I will call stand," said Sir Lachlan, in his gruff, halting tone, for he had a speech affliction. "Then steady. Then blow one trumpet blast. That is your call...to run. Anyone who goes early...is out. Anyone who interferes...with another runner...*out*."

He stared grimly down the field at the flag pole, which from here looked a thousand miles away. Next, unable to quell his curiosity, Callum glanced at the pavilion. Lady Isla stood at the front of the royal enclosure, her hands resting on the wooden frame. She did not wave, or make any movement, but he could feel that emerald gaze upon him.

"Stand!"

He tensed, his heart pounding.

"Steady!"

It seemed like forever, but a trumpet blast pierced the air, and Callum launched himself into action, his bandaged feet pounding the ground in a steady rhythm as he ran hard toward the flagpole. Soon an odd calm wrapped around him, the gasping breaths and thudding feet of his fellow runners, the yells and cheers of the crowd, all fading away to nothing. Had one man already fallen behind? He didn't dare look to confirm, not when it might cost him time or a misstep. At last, he reached the flagpole and ran around it, trying to keep his pace steady and his body as close to the pole as possible so not to cover extra distance.

God's blood, the finish line was far away.

You can do this. For Alastair and Isla.

His feet ached, his lungs burned, but Callum forced himself to charge on, the way he had as a child when chased by lads with stones and rotten fruit, calling him witch's spawn.

How much farther? My chest is going to burst.

There it is! There is the line!

He lowered his head, hurling himself forward to cross it, before tumbling onto the ground in an exhausted heap.

"Laird."

Alastair's voice pierced the fog around him, and he sat up, unsure if he could bear the answer to his question.

"Did I..." he choked out.

His squire grinned. "Aye, you damned well did. Second of five! We continue on to the archery round. But now I beseech you...accept kindness from those who offer."

Callum flopped back onto the ground. After the king had been so kind; even the thought of disobeying a royal edict made him feel ill. And sword fighting held enough bad memories to send an icy shiver down his spine.

But now that he'd met the bold and beautiful Lady Isla, talked to her and kissed her hand...he would never forgive himself if his timidity led to a bad marriage for her. There was also the fact that she liked him. Had said so. Rather than a union of cold duty, wedding such a bold and sensual woman could be rather pleasant indeed.

He took a slow, deep breath. "Very well."

CHAPTER 4

E ighteen men remained in the tourney, his laird was one of them, and he'd just agreed to accept Lady Isla's help.

Relieved beyond measure, Alastair crouched next to where Callum lay sprawled on the ground recovering his breath. In truth, he needed to recover also. Watching that race, his heart had been in his mouth the entire time. His laird had started strongly but he'd begun to tire as he rounded the flagpole, and for a few sweat-inducing moments he'd been fifth. But in the last hundred feet or so, Callum had proven to all he had the will of a champion as he passed three of the men to finish a mighty second.

"Here," he said, handing Callum the flagon of small ale he'd packed into the medicine satchel. "You've earned it."

His laird smiled gratefully as he took a gulp. "I know it was only a half mile, but it feels like I ran the length of Scotland."

"Aye, well, you're faring far better than most. The defeated twelve and their squires have left the field already; but those who remain are in varying states of health. Five have purged their stomachs, three are having their feet treated for cuts, and several are still wheezing despite finishing their race a quarter hour ago."

"Really?" said Callum, blinking.

Alastair stifled a sigh. The old laird, and that wretched Red had a lot to answer for, pecking away at Callum's spirit like two evil roosters. But he was spared the need to further comment when a liveried guard from the royal enclosure approached and inclined his head at Callum.

"Beg pardon, laird. His Grace the king, Her Grace the queen, and the Earl and Countess of Sutherland request you attend them at the pavilion so you might be recognized for your first day achievement."

"Of course," said Callum as he scrambled to his feet, and soon they all stood in front of their delighted king.

"My lords, lairds, knights, and squires," called James, resplendent in purple velvet and gold chains of state as he leaned on the wooden frame and thumped it enthusiastically. "What a magnificent day of competition, ably judged by Sir Lachlan! Twelve entrants have left us, but you remain to be celebrated for your athletic prowess. Each of you shall receive a gold coin, to be presented by Queen Margaret and Lady Isla."

All present cheered.

James smiled. "Come forward, race by race to be recognized. When you have received your reward, you may depart the field with my blessing to rest and prepare for archery on the morrow. We begin with blue."

The three successful entrants and their squires approached the pavilion. After blue came red, white, then black. Each time, the young queen dressed in ermine-lined satin and blood-red rubies, placed a gold coin in their palm before holding out her hand to be bowed over. Then the men were permitted to share a brief conversation with Lady Isla.

She wore a dark green gown and jewel-studded silver girdle, but he could sense her displeasure and discomfort at wearing it. Poor lass. One of Callum's embroidered linen shirts and a pair of fine hose would fit much better. There was little doubt in his mind that her arse would rival Callum's in perfection, and then he could admire both.

"Yellow race!" called James.

As the victor, Red was recognized first with his gold coin, and when he murmured something to the queen, she blushed and giggled. Then he moved to Lady Isla, deliberately taking her hand and kissing it as they conversed.

Alastair and Callum both tensed. However, with all eyes on them, revealing their true feelings would do them no favor. To everyone else, Red behaved in the manner of a gallant. The queen certainly viewed his actions as appropriate. But when he turned and smirked at Alastair and Callum, it was clear he'd done it to annoy them rather than gain favor with the ladies.

Devil-spawned gutter rat.

"Green race!"

The border lord who had won the race went first, and seemed to converse with the queen and Lady Isla for a thousand years. But at last, Alastair and Callum strode forward.

"Glennoe!" said the king with a friendly smile. "What a strong finish. I look forward to seeing your archery. You prepared your laird well, Master Graham."

His cheeks heated at the praise. "Thank you, Your Grace."

They each received their gold coin from the queen and bowed over her hand, but he was impatient to speak with Lady Isla, and knew Callum wished to also.

"Glennoe," said Lady Isla, her smile bright, even as her gaze remained uncertain. "Master Graham. I am most impressed, even if a foot race is not my favorite Highland pastime. I fear I would not have even finished it. Tell me, what would you advise a body who had the heart and the desire, but not quite the skill to win?"

Alastair went still, silently urging his laird to accept the offer previously made.

Callum's brow furrowed. "An interesting question, Lady Isla. My counsel would be to find someone who is greatly skilled and humbly request assistance without delay. To be the best, you must learn from the best."

Her face lit up. "Sound advice. Should I begin this day?"

"Indeed. Forgive us, but Master Graham and I must retire to our cottage to rest. There is much to prepare."

Lady Isla nodded solemnly and held out her hand. "I wish you good fortune. And you, Master Graham."

Callum kissed her hand and moved to one side, then Alastair took her hand in his.

Plague take it, her palm was slightly rough with healed calluses. The flesh of a true swordfighter. He would give anything to be able to kiss her as Callum had, but a squire had no such leave.

Her palms might be rough, but those adorable small breasts would be soft as satin. Her inner thighs even softer. As for the slick folds of her cunt, rose petals would weep in envy.

A soft growl escaped at the thought of discovering such treasures, and Lady Isla shivered, her hand briefly rubbing against his. Almost groaning at the sweet friction, Alastair stepped back, bowed, and joined Callum to walk back to the cottage.

After their exertions in the sun and noise of a large crowd, the cool stillness was most welcome. The larder had been restocked, and Alastair eagerly downed two still-warm meat pasties, and a thick slice of fruit cake. In the other room he could hear Callum stoking the fire and pouring water, no doubt preparing a salted bath for his abused feet. "Are you hungry?"

"At this moment I could eat an entire banquet," came the rueful reply.

Smiling, Alastair prepared a tray of food and a goblet of wine, then carried them into the main room. Callum stood watching the water heating over the fire, both hands braced on the stone shelf, his weariness evident.

"You should sit," he chided.

"I fear if I sit, I'll never get up again," said Callum, as he took three slices of buttered bread and honey and devoured them as though he'd not eaten for a week. Two meat pasties, a handful of dried fruit, some almond comfits, and the entire goblet of wine soon followed.

Alastair put his hand on Callum's shoulder, intending to guide him onto the chaise near the fire. "Rest," he growled.

His laird went rigid. "Don't...I'm clinging to my resolve by the thinnest of threads."

"Are you?"

Callum shuddered, and those silver-gray eyes widened in need, his expression pure yearning. "I am weary after the race. But I also find myself feeling...restless. A need to touch and be touched. I know I ask far too much after I pushed you away, but...would you kiss me, Alastair?"

Lust surged through him, more powerful than the rush of a waterfall. Between his frustrated desire for Lady Isla and the hot, rough, wickedly good acts he wanted to do once again to this man...

Instead, he nodded. "Aye."

Slowly, so slowly, for although his laird had expressed the need he still had an air of skittishness about him, Alastair cupped Callum's face and brushed his lips against the younger man's. Then he gently flicked his tongue until Callum permitted him entry to his mouth. His laird tasted sweet and heady like wine, and desire jolted through him, hardening his cock to stone.

At the stealthy slide of Callum's hands under his shirt to rest on his chest, those slender, nimble fingers stroking the wiry hair and teasing his nipples, Alastair groaned. In retribution, he dropped his hands to Callum's tight arse, then began grinding his hose-covered cock against the rapidly hardening bulge of his laird's.

Callum gasped, the sound echoing in the room. "More."

"Of what, laird?" he murmured, leaning down to nip the other man's shoulder. "Tell me...*exactly*."

"Pleasure," said Callum hoarsely. "Your hands and mouth on me until I gain release. It's been so long. Please..."

"I'm going to taste every inch of you. Then I'm going to fuck you so hard and deep you'll feel me for days."

"Now?"

Alastair nodded, ushering him across to the chaise. "Yes. Now."

⚜

"Are ye sure about this, lassie? There'll be grave trouble should anyone find out where ye truly are."

Isla smiled reassuringly at Morag and her husband Leith, the two middle-aged treasures who had quietly assisted more rebellions than anyone knew. As longtime Sutherland servants, the childless couple had taken her under their wing; Morag soothing upsets and scolding foolishness, Leith presenting her with the most cherished gift of her childhood: a little wooden sword. He'd also taught her how to hold it correctly and move her feet. Really, she loved them far more than her own mother and father. While they had come to Stirling because of Morag's unmatched sewing ability and Leith's position as chief messenger, she needed them for a different purpose entirely.

"As far as anyone knows, I am perusing the market in Stirling with trusted servants. Now you can visit your sister, Morag, and when the time comes to return to the castle for supper, I'll be waiting here for you."

Morag didn't look fully convinced, nor did Leith. But they nodded and continued down the path to the village.

Glancing both ways to ensure no one watched, Isla straightened her shoulders and approached the front door of Glennoe's cottage. Leith knew where all the tourney entrants were lodged—he'd had to deliver messages at various times—and this information was proving invaluable, for she hadn't needed to ask anyone and create suspicion.

She raised her hand to knock, but the door wasn't properly latched and swung open. Not wanting to be seen loitering, Isla stepped inside the cool stone building and latched the door behind her.

Just about to call a cheerful greeting, the words died in her throat.

Saints alive.

At first glance, it appeared that a seated Master Graham attended to a small wound on his half-naked laird's lower belly or hip. But no. Glennoe's hose rested about his knees. His hands were braced on his squire's shoulders, his head tilted back in ecstasy as his fully erect cock was roughly handled.

Saints ALIVE.

Isla had seen cocks before; the lads in her training group had never been shy when needing to relieve themselves, or for a jest. But a grown man's? At full mast? Never.

She sank against the wall, unable to tear her gaze away from the shockingly erotic sight of one man pleasuring another, for now Master Graham teased Glennoe's cock with long, slow laps of his tongue, before engulfing the entire head in his mouth.

The laird made a sound of such delight that Isla scarcely